ARTHUR and the DRAGON

Written by Pauline Cartwright
Illustrated by David Elliot

Arthur Littlejohn had been taught to be a very careful person.
Even when he was a grown-up man of considerable years,
he was still being so careful that he had never had an adventure.

Then came the day that he found the enormous egg. Arthur felt
a sudden unfamiliar fizz of excitement at the sight of it.

The egg, with its silvery sheen,
was lying in the pines where Arthur often went for an evening walk.
Careful Arthur was going to walk right past it,
without even touching it,
but the fizzing excitement inside him changed his mind.
The egg was so big, Arthur had to put both arms around it
to carry it home.

Inside, he put the egg down gently on the carpet.
Something would hatch from this wonderful egg and he, Arthur Littlejohn, would be the first to know what that something was.

Each day, he rolled the egg very gently over by the windows
where the autumn sun could stroke it with warm yellow fingers.
At day's end, when the edge of a frosty evening started sliding in,
Arthur Littlejohn lit his fire.
He rolled the egg back from the window to where the firelight
could dance an orange dance on its shell.

In spite of the careful watch he kept,
Arthur didn't see the egg hatch.
One morning,he found that the great shell
had cracked open while he'd been sleeping. There in the middle of the room
stood a lizard-like creature, sky-blue with silver-tipped wings
and a silver-edged tail.
Her eyes were a deep inky blue.
Arthur knew she was a creature belonging to magical places.

"I shall call you Amanda," said Mr. Arthur Littlejohn.
The sky-blue creature stared at Arthur.
Then she spread her silver-tipped wings and glided onto his shoulder.
There she stayed nearly all day, snuggling her snout
under the lapel of his jacket when she wanted to sleep.

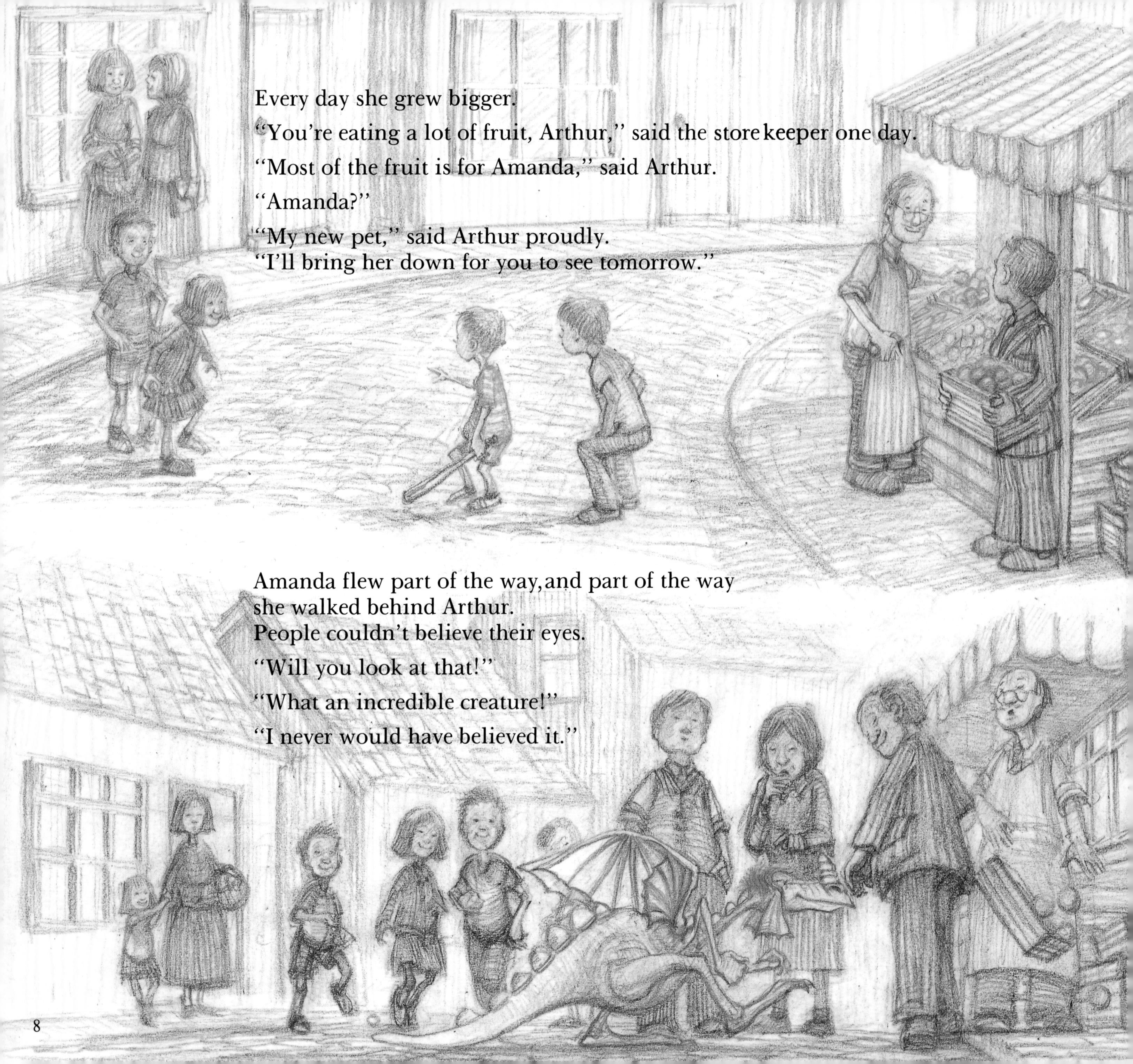

Every day she grew bigger.

"You're eating a lot of fruit, Arthur," said the storekeeper one day.

"Most of the fruit is for Amanda," said Arthur.

"Amanda?"

"My new pet," said Arthur proudly.
"I'll bring her down for you to see tomorrow."

Amanda flew part of the way, and part of the way
she walked behind Arthur.
People couldn't believe their eyes.

"Will you look at that!"

"What an incredible creature!"

"I never would have believed it."

They followed Arthur and Amanda down the street
and crowded around them at the grocery store.
Amanda, who was getting too big to sit on Arthur's shoulder, flew up and sat on top of the fruit stand.

"Where did you get it?"

"What are you going to do with it?"

"What *is* it?"

It made Arthur feel very important answering all the questions.
But he didn't answer the last one.
Amanda, he knew, was a dragon, a quiet and gentle dragon from magical places.
Some people believed all dragons were fearsome things.

He called Amanda down so that people could softly touch the silver tips of her wings and stroke the sky-blue scales on her back.
A baby climbed on Amanda's back, poking at her ears. Amanda didn't mind.

"I think she's lovely."

"I'd like a pet like that myself."

The townsfolk liked Amanda, and she liked them.

Arthur had never had a lot of visitors, but from that day on
there was often someone climbing the hill to visit him,
bringing an orange or an apple for his pet.
Children came,too,and went for short flights on Amanda's back.
When Arthur went on his way to the shops,
people came out of their houses and gardens to pat his dragon pet.

Then one morning when Arthur came downstairs, he was amazed to find that not only had Amanda doubled in size overnight, but she had become truly dragonish in another way. Small warm flames huffed from her nostrils.

"I think," said Arthur to Amanda, "that people are going to notice this."

They did.

"That creature of yours," said one visitor, "is a *dragon*!"

"I know," said Arthur.

"You *know*!"

"Dragons are dangerous! You can't keep a dangerous pet!"

"She's not a dangerous pet," protested Arthur.
"She's Amanda, gentle Amanda who takes your children for rides
and who lies in the sun while you stroke her back and feed her oranges."

Amanda kept growing.
Soon she was too big to come into Arthur's house.
He parked the car on the street so that she could sleep
in the garage. When he felt lonely at night, he crept out
and slept in the fold of her front legs, under her fiery snout
where it was pleasantly warm.

Eventually Amanda grew so large that at night the garage door had to be left open. Her long tail stretched outside and curved comfortably around the house wall.

The people who used to come and see her didn't come anymore.

"No one should be allowed to keep an animal like that."

"The fire in its nostrils is terrifying!"

"It's become so big that when it flies about town,
it shuts out all the sunlight."

Arthur couldn't take Amanda down the street for walks anymore.
People complained about the room she took up
and that she singed the flower beds when she looked over the fences.
One man even complained that she had eaten his dog!

"She eats fruit and carrots and cheese," protested Arthur,
"not dogs. She's stopped growing now and even though she's big,
she's just as gentle as she was before. You must believe me."

Even when the man's dog came home
(it wasn't very well-behaved and had run away for a few days),
people still kept talking about the terrible dragon that ate dogs.
They started wondering when it would begin to eat people.

Instead of daytime walks, Arthur and Amanda now went for long flights at night over the sleeping town, swooping in and out of the clouds in the same way that a seal swoops through water. During the day they stayed home.

Neighbors wanted Arthur to put a high fence around his property. The town clerk, who needed money to repair the sidewalks, was trying to get the Mayor to make Arthur pay a special dragon-keeping license of an exorbitant amount. Amanda hadn't done anything fearsome, but no one believed in her gentleness anymore.

Finally, a long line of people carrying banners that said things like:
KEEP TOWNS FOR PEOPLE NOT DRAGONS and
BAN MAN-EATING ANIMALS,
delivered a petition to the council saying that no one should be allowed to keep a dragon as a pet.
The council held a meeting and agreed to make a new law saying that the keeping of dragons was forbidden.
A copy was sent to Mr. Littlejohn.
Amanda had to be gone in ten days.

Arthur cried. "I know you have places to go, Amanda.
Dragonish places where you will be very happy.
But I will miss you very, very much.
Life with you is a wonderful adventure."

Amanda turned her head to nuzzle Arthur,
and suddenly through his tears Arthur saw that her eyes
were saying, "Come with me. Come with me to magic dragonish places
where no one is frightened because things are big.
Come with me and let life keep on being an adventure."

"Could I?" said Arthur. "Could I really?"

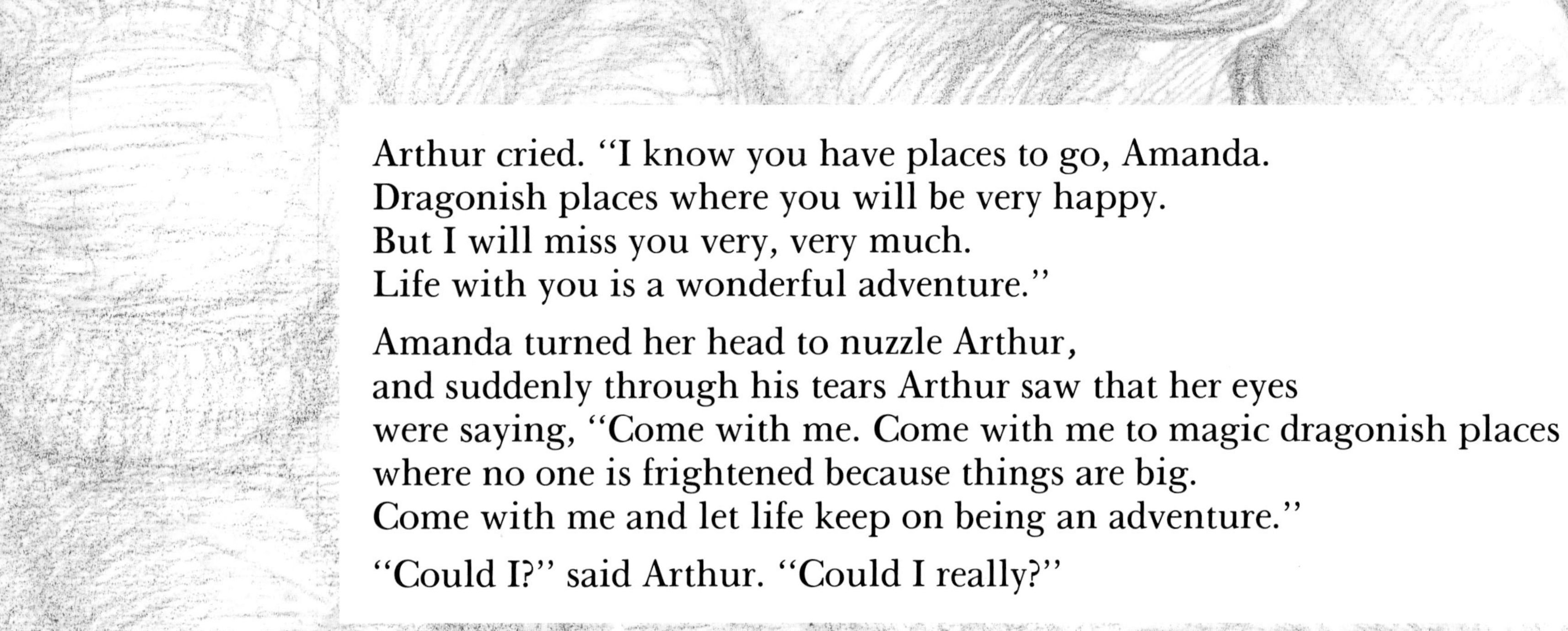

There and then, Arthur decided he would.
That night they celebrated with a long soaring flight,sweeping through the stars and in and out of moonbeams until Arthur's head spun.

Sleeping late in the morning, they didn't hear the rain begin.
By the time they woke,it was pouring down.
It kept pouring for two days and two nights,
pouring and pouring so that the river
running through the town began to fill with swirling muddy water.

Up in the mountains it had been raining for even longer.
Down came the rainwater from the mountains,filling the river even more.
Higher and higher it rose. Then,before the people of the town
realized it was going to happen, over the banks came the water,
pouring into the streets and poking wet fingers under doors.

Inside houses people put couches on tables. The water kept coming.
They put bookcases on top of the couches.
They stacked valuable objects higher still.
Then they tried wading to high ground, but the water was getting too deep.

They climbed onto rooftops and waited to be saved.
Dogs were howling and chickens squawking.
The Mayor leaned out of the top story of the council building
and called for everyone with boats to bring them
to the rescue of the town.

"Amanda," said Arthur, looking down from their hilltop house,
"it's time for us to help."

When the sky-blue dragon with the silver-tipped wings flew down to the town, not one person cried, "Look out for the fierce dragon." Instead they called, "Amanda! Save us,Amanda!"

And that is just what Amanda did.
People climbed on her back and sat in rows.
She flew them, one load after another, to Arthur's hilltop where the floodwaters couldn't reach.
Some slept in Arthur's house, some in the neighbors' houses, and some made shelters in the pines.
There they stayed until the rain stopped and the waters went down.

Arthur had been given ten days to remove Amanda from the town.
By that time, the floodwaters had receded,
and Amanda had been up and down the streets
breathing warm, dragon flames,
drying out the houses.
The townsfolk were back in their homes, cozy and dry again.

Realizing how foolish they had been, they began visiting Arthur and Amanda again, bringing fruit and carrots.

So it was that a group of visitors came upon Arthur clutching a suitcase in one hand and about to climb on Amanda's back. They could see that his house was firmly locked up.

"Where are you going?" they asked in surprise.

"The law in this town forbids dragons.
So Amanda is leaving, and I am going, too.
We are flying far away to magic dragonish places,
where no one is frightened because things are big."

In the excitement of floods and dragon rescues and house-cleaning, the people had forgotten about the law they had forced the council to make, and they were ashamed.

"Please don't go!"

"The law says Amanda must," said Arthur. "I want to be with her." He climbed on the dragon's back. "You could ask the council to change the law. Then we could come back for visits."

"We could," cried the people. "We could."

A little man at the back suddenly said,
"I don't know if that would be wise. Some dragons *are* fierce,you know.
We should be careful about these things."

"Oh, indeed," said Arthur, although the people were
too busy arguing to hear him. "You need to be careful."

He looked at the little man and thought he didn't look unlike himself.
"But not too careful," added Arthur. "Not *too* careful."

He settled himself more comfortably on Amanda's back, and off they flew while the people argued.

High into the sky they flew,
beyond all the yesterdays and into the edges of tomorrow,
to magic dragonish places, where adventures happen
at least once a week.